Bella Learns To Ball

By Jake Beaman

Illustrations by Alegria and Omayra Michael

Copyright © 2019
By Jake Beaman
Illustrations by Alegria and Omayra Michael
Bella Learns To Ball
All rights reserved.

No part of this publication may be reproduced, distributed, or transmitted in any form or by any means, including photocopying, recording, or other electronic or mechanical methods, without the prior written permission of the publisher, except in the case of brief quotations embodied in critical reviews and certain other non-commercial uses permitted by copyright law.

By Jake Beaman
Illustrations by Alegria and Omayra Michael

Printed in the United States of America
First Printing 2019
First Edition 2019

10 9 8 7 6 5 4 3 2 1

This book is dedicated to our daughter Isabella and written for anyone with a dream to ball.

Table of Contents

This book belongs to:

_____

Bella Learns To Ball

Chapter 1

1

Bella learns to ball

Before she's even 3 feet tall

Although her hands may be small

Her parents found a ball

3

Bella went to practice to shoot

As her Dad cheered, "WOOT WOOT"

5

Bella practiced moving her feet

With her Mom up and down the street

7

Bella dreamed she jumped like a kangaroo

As her parents whispered, "Goodnight I love you!"

9

In her dream the crowd cheered as she ran on the court

And she woke up excited to practice her favorite sport

Bella asked her dad,

"Who's the best to ever ball?"

Her dad explained, "Well that's a hard call"...

13

In the 60's

Wilt was tall as a stilt

Who scored 100 points when the NBA was first built

Bill won the most rings

Because he could do all the little things

15

In the 70's

Kareem could score at almost every shot he took

With a shot hard to guard called the sky hook

In the 80's

Magic and Larry saved the NBA

One the best passer and the other could shoot all day

17

In the 90's

Jordan had the best kicks and most say is the greatest of all time

Because he could score at will and even dunk from the free throw line

19

We had Kobe and Shaq

Who were the most feared

Guard and big man attack

21

Candace and Lisa two bigs that can dunk down the lane

Diana's a guard with a shot nice enough to make it rain

23

Today in the league we have Lebron

who's strength and consistency changed the game

Making a chase down block that led to ultimate fame

Steph can shoot from anywhere on the court

He changes a defenses entire scouting report

Bella stayed up late and thought about all the greats

She decided she wanted to shoot like Curry

"Practice hard" her dad said, "but not in a hurry"

25

Chapter 2

To perfect your shot and continue to improve

Shoot day after day to find your perfect groove

Bella practiced her shot in the sun and the rain

She even brought her ball on an airplane

29

Day after day she continued to play

Practicing with friends getting better each day

Bella scored baskets at the park

As her Dog cheered and barked

31

Bella even went to the fair

And won prizes everywhere

33

Now it was finally time to play on a team

She was so nervous she could scream

In a game with refs and whistles how would she play?

She wondered would her teammates like her okay?

34

35

To start the game Bella missed shot after shot

"This is Impossible!" She thought

Her Mom assured her to just be calm and play her game

Bella already succeeded

She did the hard work when she trained

This game would never be the real test

What counts is preparing and giving it your best

Chapter 3

On the next play when Bella got the ball she passed it to a teammate like Magic

And her teammate scored a basket dribbling through traffic

41

She soared like Jordan for a buzzer beater shot

All her teammates gave her high fives

As she strolled down the court in a trot

43

She carefully guarded the other team like Kawhi

As her coach cheered, "you're doing great, give it your best try"

The next play the pass hit her hands and she dropped the ball

She began to panic but remembered what mattered most

"Just give it your all"

45

Now it was almost the end of the game and the score was close

Coach said, "Were down 1 point, this is when you concentrate most"

With 1 second left Bella got the ball up top

She took a breath and put up the shot

Time seemed to slow as the ball floated in the air

Swishhhhh the ball went through the net as the crowd screamed from everywhere

She hugged her teammates and high fived the other team

She made the game winner and it seemed like a perfect dream

49

She had practiced and practiced shooting the ball

Her hard work is what mattered most of all

Her parents were so proud she practiced and gave it her best

Now get some sleep tonight; 3 pointers tomorrow will be the new test

51

The End

Made in the USA
Monee, IL
16 August 2022

11716985R00036